wishtree

wishtree

katherine applegate

Illustrated by Charles Santoso

Feiwel and Friends
New York

A FEIWEL AND FRIENDS BOOK
An imprint of Macmillan Publishing Group, LLC
175 Fifth Avenue, New York, NY 10010

Our books may be purchased in bulk for promotional, educational, or
business use. Please contact your local bookseller or the Macmillan Corporate
and Premium Sales Department at (800) 221-7945 ext. 5442 or by e-mail at
MacmillanSpecialMarkets@macmillan.com.

Library of Congress Cataloging-in-Publication Data

Names: Applegate, Katherine, author.
Title: Wishtree / Katherine Applegate.
Description: First edition. | New York : Feiwel and Friends, 2017. | Summary: An old
    red oak tree tells how along with crow friend, Bongo, they help their human
    neighbors get along after a threat against an immigrant family is carved into
    the tree's trunk.
Identifiers: LCCN 2016058768 (print) | LCCN 2017029142 (ebook) | ISBN
    9781250143037 (Ebook) | ISBN 9781250043221 (hardcover)
Subjects: | CYAC: Toleration—Fiction. | Trees—Fiction. | Crows—Fiction. |
    Wishes—Fiction. | Friendship—Fiction.
Classification: LCC PZ7.A6483 (ebook) | LCC PZ7.A6483 Wis 2017 (print) |
    DDC [Fic]—dc23
LC record available at https://lccn.loc.gov/2016058768

Book design by Liz Dresner

Feiwel and Friends logo designed by Filomena Tuosto

First edition, 2017

20   19   18   17   16   15   14   13

mackids.com

for newcomers
and
for welcomers

Be Different to Trees

The talking oak
To the ancients spoke.
But any tree
Will talk to me.
What truths I know
I garnered so.
But those who want to talk and tell,
*   And those who will not listeners be,*
Will never hear a syllable
*   From out the lips of any tree.*

—MARY CAROLYN DAVIES (1924)

1

It's hard to talk to trees. We're not big on chitchat.

That's not to say we can't do amazing things, things you'll probably never do.

Cradle downy owlets. Steady flimsy tree forts. Photosynthesize.

But talk to people? Not so much.

And just try to get a tree to tell a good joke.

Trees do talk to some folks, the ones we know we

can trust. We talk to daredevil squirrels. We talk to hardworking worms. We talk to flashy butterflies and bashful moths.

Birds? They're delightful. Frogs? Grumpy, but good-hearted. Snakes? Terrible gossips.

Trees? Never met a tree I didn't like.

Well, okay. There's that sycamore down at the corner. Yakkity-yakkity-yak, that one.

So do we ever talk to people? Actually *talk*, that most people-y of people skills?

Good question.

Trees have a rather complicated relationship with people, after all. One minute you're hugging us. The next minute you're turning us into tables and tongue depressors.

Perhaps you're wondering why the fact that trees talk wasn't covered in science class, during those *Mother Nature Is Our Friend* lessons.

Don't blame your teachers. They probably don't know that trees can talk. Most people don't.

Nonetheless, if you find yourself standing near

a particularly friendly-looking tree on a particularly lucky-feeling day, it can't hurt to listen up.

Trees can't tell jokes.

But we can certainly tell stories.

And if all you hear is the whisper of leaves, don't worry. Most trees are introverts at heart.

2

Name's Red, by the way.

Maybe we've met? Oak tree near the elementary school? Big, but not too? Sweet shade in the summer, fine color in the fall?

I am proud to say that I'm a northern red oak, also known as *Quercus rubra*. Red oaks are one of the most common trees in North America. In my neighborhood alone, hundreds upon hundreds of us are weaving our roots into the soil like knitters on a mission.

I have ridged, reddish-gray bark; leathery leaves with pointed lobes; stubborn, searching roots; and, if I do say so myself, the best fall color on the street. "Red" doesn't begin to do me justice. Come October, I look like I'm ablaze. It's a miracle the fire department doesn't try to hose me down every autumn.

You might be surprised to learn that all red oaks are named Red.

Likewise, all sugar maples are called Sugar. All junipers are called Juniper. And all boojum trees are called Boojum.

That's how it is in tree world. We don't need names to tell one another apart.

Imagine a classroom where every child is named

Melvin. Imagine the poor teacher trying to take attendance each morning.

It's a good thing trees don't go to school.

Of course, there are exceptions to the name rule. Somewhere in Los Angeles there's a palm tree who insists on being called Karma, but you know how Californians can be.

3

My friends call me Red, and you can, too. But for a long time people in the neighborhood have called me the "wishtree."

There's a reason for this, and it goes way back to when I wasn't much more than a tiny seed with higher aspirations.

Long story.

Every year on the first day of May, people come

from all over town to adorn me with scraps of paper, tags, bits of fabric, snippets of yarn, and the occasional gym sock. Each offering represents a dream, a desire, a longing.

Whether draped, tossed, or tied with a bow: They're all hopes for something better.

Wishtrees have a long and honorable history, going back centuries. There are many in Ireland, where they are usually hawthorns or the occasional ash tree. But you can find wishtrees all over the world.

For the most part, people are kind when they visit me. They seem to understand that a tight knot might keep me from growing the way I need to grow. They are gentle with my new leaves, careful with my exposed roots.

After people write their hope on a rag or piece of paper, they tie it onto one of my branches. Usually they whisper the wish aloud.

It's traditional to wish on the first of May, but people stop by throughout the year.

My, oh my, the things I have heard:

I wish for a flying skateboard.

I wish for a world without war.

I wish for a week without clouds.

I wish for the world's biggest candy bar.

I wish for an A on my geography test.

I wish Ms. Gentorini weren't so grumpy in the morning.

I wish my gerbil could talk.

I wish my dad could get better.

I wish I weren't hungry sometimes.

I wish I weren't so lonely.

I wish I knew what to wish for.

So many wishes. Grand and goofy, selfish and sweet.

It's an honor, all the hopes bestowed upon my tired old limbs.

Although by the end of May Day, I look like someone dumped a huge basket of trash on top of me.

4

As you've probably noticed, I'm more talkative than most trees. This is new for me. I'm still getting the hang of it.

Nonetheless, I've always known how to keep a secret. You have to be discreet when you're a wishtree.

People tell trees all kinds of things. They know we'll listen.

It's not like we have a choice.

Besides, the more you listen, the more you learn.

Bongo says I'm a busybody, and I suppose she has a point. She's my best pal, a crow I've known since she was nothing but a pecking beak in a speckled egg.

We disagree sometimes, but that is the way of all friends, no matter their species. I've seen many surprising friendships during my life: a pony and a toad, a red-tailed hawk and a white-footed mouse, a lilac bush and a monarch butterfly. All of them had disagreements from time to time.

I think Bongo is too pessimistic for such a young bird.

Bongo thinks I'm too optimistic for such an old tree.

It's true. I am an optimist. I prefer to take the long view on life. Old as I am, I've seen both good and bad. But I've seen far more good than bad.

So Bongo and I agree to disagree. And that's fine. We're very different, after all.

Bongo, for example, thinks the way we trees name ourselves is ridiculous. As is the custom with crows, Bongo chose her name after her first flight. It may not be her only name, however. Crows change names on a whim. Bongo's cousin, Gizmo, has had seventeen names.

Sometimes crows adopt human names; I've seen more Joe Crows than I've seen sunny days. Sometimes they name themselves after things that catch their fancy: Poptop, Jujube, DeadRat. They'll name themselves after aerobatic maneuvers: DeathSpiral or BarrelRoll. Or after colors: Aubergine or BeetleBlack.

Many crows opt for sounds they're fond of making. (Crows are excellent mimics.) I've met crows named WindChime, EighteenWheeler, and GrouchyCabDriver, not to mention a few others that are not appropriate for polite company.

Down the street lives an aspiring rock band composed of four middle schoolers. They practice in a garage. Their instruments include an accordion, a bass guitar, a tuba, and bongo drums.

The band has yet to perform outside of the garage, but Bongo loves to sit on the roof and sway to their music.

5

Names aren't the only way we differ from crows.

Some trees are male. Some trees are female. And some, like me, are both.

It's confusing, as is so often the case with nature.

Call me she. Call me he. Anything will work.

Over the years, I've learned that botanists—those lucky souls who study the lives of plants all day—call some trees, such as hollies and willows, "dioecious," which means they have separate male and female trees.

Lots of other trees, like me, are called "monoecious." That's just a fancy way of saying that on the same plant you'll find separate male and female flowers.

It is also evidence that trees have far more interesting lives than you sometimes give us credit for.

6

One thing trees and crows have in common—
in fact, one thing all the natural world has in
common—is the rule that we're not supposed to talk
to people.

It's for our own protection. At least that's the
theory.

I've often wondered if the endless silence is a
good idea. There've been so many times I've wanted

to speak up, to intervene, to help people. I've never said a word, though. That's just the way the world has always worked.

Have there been slip-ups? Sure, mistakes have been made.

Last year I heard about a frog named Fly, who'd been napping in a mailbox. (All frogs are named after bugs they enjoy eating.) When the mailman opened the box, Fly leapt out with a frantic croak. The mailman fainted.

He woke up to Fly, who was apologizing profusely, squatting on his forehead.

Clearly, a breach of the *Don't Talk to People* rule.

But as always seems to happen, the incident was soon forgotten. After all, the mailman was absolutely certain that frogs can't talk. "Just hearing things," he no doubt told himself.

Interestingly enough, he retired not long after the frog incident.

In any case, when you consider the number of trees and frogs and otters and wrens and dragonflies and armadillos and everybody else in the natural world, you'd think people would have caught on to our little secret by now.

What can I say? Nature is tricky. And people are . . . well, sorry, but most of you aren't that observant.

Perhaps you're wondering, if you're a curious or doubting sort, just exactly how trees communicate. You may find yourself inspecting a nearby ponderosa pine, perhaps, or an aspen or sweet gum, puzzling out the magic.

People speak with the help of lungs, throats, voice boxes, tongues, and lips, thanks to an intricate symphony of sound and breath and movement.

But there are plenty of other ways to convey information. An eyebrow cocked, a giggle stifled, a tear brushed aside: These, too, are ways you express yourself.

For a tree, communication is just as complicated and miraculous as it is for humans. In a mysterious dance of sunlight and sugar, water and wind and soil, we build invisible bridges to connect with the world.

21

Frogs have their own ways of connecting. Same for dogs. Same for newts and spiders, elephants and eagles.

How exactly do we do it? That's for us to know and you to figure out.

Nature also adores a good secret.

7

I'm not just a tree, by the way. I'm a home. A community.

Folks nest on my branches. Burrow between my roots. Lay eggs on my leaves.

And then there are my hollows. Tree hollows—holes in a trunk or branch—are not uncommon, especially in trees like me who've been around awhile.

Hollows can be small enough for tiny salt-and-pepper chickadees or a family of deer mice. Or they can be quite large, big enough for an open-minded bear.

Of course, I'm a city tree. We don't get a lot of bears around here, unless they're of the teddy variety. But I've hosted more than my share of raccoons, foxes, skunks, opossums, and mice. One year I was home to a lovely and exceedingly polite porcupine family.

I've even sheltered a person.

Long story. (I have lots of those, stored up the way a squirrel hoards acorns.)

Hollows happen for many reasons. Woodpeckers. Fallen branches. Lightning. Disease. Burrowing insects.

In my case, I have three hollows. Two medium-sized ones were made by woodpeckers. The largest one happened when I was quite young. I lost a large branch that was weakened by wet snow during a nor'easter. It was a big wound, slow to heal, and my spring leafing that year was paltry, my fall color pale (and, frankly, embarrassing).

But eventually the hole healed, widened with the help of insects, and now, about four feet off the ground, I have a deep oval hollow.

Hollows offer protection from the elements. A secure spot to sleep and to stash your belongings. They're a safe place.

Hollows are proof that something bad can become something good with enough time and care and hope.

Being a home to others isn't always easy. Sometimes I feel like an apartment complex with too many residents. Residents who don't always get along.

Still, we make it work. There's a lot of give-and-take in nature. Woodpeckers hammer at my trunk, but they also eat annoying pests. Grass cools the earth, but it also bickers with me over water.

Every spring brings new residents, old friends, and more chances for compromise. This spring in particular has seen quite the baby boom. Currently, I am home to owl nestlings, baby opossums, and tiny raccoons. I am also visited regularly by the skunk kits who live underneath the front porch of a nearby house.

This is unprecedented. Never have I sheltered so many babies. It just doesn't happen. Animals like space. They like their own territory. Normally, there would be arguing. Perhaps even a stolen nest or a midnight battle.

And certainly, there've been some disagreements. But I've made it clear that eating your neighbors will not be allowed while I'm in charge.

Me, I don't feel crowded at all having so much company.

Making others feel safe is a fine way to spend your days.

8

I have one more community member, although "visitor" is probably a better way to describe Samar.

In January, she moved with her parents into one of the houses I shade, a tiny blue house with a sagging porch and a tidy garden. She is perhaps ten years old or so, with wary eyes and a shy smile.

Samar has the look of someone who has seen too much. Someone who wants the world to quiet itself.

Soon after moving in, Samar began sneaking into the yard once her parents had fallen asleep. Even on the coldest nights, she trudged outside in her red boots and green jacket. Her breath was a frosty veil. She would stare at the moon, and at me, and sometimes, at the little green house next door, where a boy who looks to be about her age lives.

As it grew warmer, Samar would venture out in her pajamas and robe and sit beneath me on an old blanket, spattered with moonlight. Her silence was so complete, her gentleness so apparent, that the residents would crawl from their nests of thistledown and dandelion fluff to join her. They seemed to accept her as one of their own.

Bongo especially loved Samar. She would flit to her shoulder and settle there. Sometimes she would say "hello," in a fine imitation of Samar's voice.

Often Bongo gave Samar little gifts she'd found during her daily flights. A Monopoly token (the car). A gold hair ribbon. A cap from a root beer bottle.

Bongo keeps a stash of odds and ends in one of

my smaller hollows (which the opossums kindly tolerate). "You never know who I might need to bribe," she likes to say.

But her gifts to Samar weren't bribes. They were just Bongo's way of saying, "I'm glad we're friends."

If this were a fairy tale, I would tell you there was something magical about Samar. That she cast a spell on the animals, perhaps. Animals don't just leave their nests and burrows willingly. They are afraid of people, with good reason.

But this isn't a fairy tale, and there was no spell.

Animals compete for resources, just like humans. They eat one another. They fight for dominance.

Nature is not always pretty or fair or kind.

But sometimes surprises happen. And Samar, every spring night, reminded me there is beauty in stillness and grace in acceptance.

And that you're never too old to be surprised.

9

I was pleased to see Samar's family join the neighborhood. It had been a long while since we'd had any newcomers. But I knew that with time they would put down roots, just like so many other families from so many other places.

I know a thing or two about roots.

One night not long ago, Samar came out to visit. It was two in the morning. Late, even for her.

She had been crying. Her cheeks were damp. She leaned against me and her tears were like hot rain.

In her hand was a small piece of cloth. Pink with little dots. Something was written on it.

A wish. The first wish I'd seen in months.

I wasn't surprised she knew about the wishtree tradition. I'm kind of a local celebrity.

Samar reached up, gently pulled down my lowest branch, and tied the fabric in a loose knot.

"I wish," she whispered, "for a friend."

She glanced over at the green house. Behind an upstairs curtain, a shadow moved.

And with that, Samar vanished back into the little blue house.

10

When you stand still for over two centuries while the world whirls past, things happen.

Mostly, by far and away, good things have been my lot in life. My leaves have cooled picnickers and proposers. Beneath my boughs vows have been made, hearts mended. Nappers have napped; dreamers have dreamed. I've watched ascents attempted, listened to stories spun.

And the laughter! Always and forever, laughter.

But sometimes things happen that aren't so good. When they occur, I've learned that there's not much you can do except stand tall and reach deep.

I have, for example, been hacked at, carved into, used for target practice.

I have been underwatered, overpruned, fertilized and fussed over, ignored and neglected. I have been struck by lightning, battered by sleet.

I have been threatened with axes, chainsaws, diseases, and insects.

I have tolerated the sharp claws of squirrels and the nagging pokes of woodpeckers. I have been climbed by cats and marked by dogs.

I have my aches and pains, like everyone. Last year I had a mite infestation that drove me nuts. Leaf blister, sooty mold, oak wilt, leaf scorch: Been there, done that.

Still, trees are luckier than people in one way. Only one percent of a fully grown tree is actually alive at any one time. Most of me is made of wood cells that are no longer living. In many ways, that makes me tougher than you.

So, yes. I've seen a lot. And who knows? I may see much more. I could live to be three hundred, five hundred, even. It happens. Red oaks lead long lives, longer than our daintier friends black willows, persimmons, apples, and redbuds.

And yet, a few days after Samar's tearful wish, something happened that made me wonder if I'd finally witnessed too much.

11

The morning was budding, and I was waiting for warmth. Down the street, a lanky boy was lingering near a stop sign.

Head down, he was hunched over like a wind-blown weed. In his right hand was something shiny. A tool, maybe, or a pen.

He was smiling just a bit, as if he'd told himself a joke. A joke only he, perhaps, understood.

All day long I see people lost in thought, talking to themselves, grinning, frowning. He was nothing out of the ordinary.

I was in the midst of a conversation with Bongo, who had just pointed out to me that I was a year older. Two hundred and sixteen rings old, to be precise.

"Another sproutday," I said. "I still feel like a sapling."

"You don't look a day over a hundred and fifty," Bongo replied. "Best-looking tree on the block."

"I'm really"—I paused for comic effect—"getting up there."

Bongo, who was perched on my lowest branch, sighed. A crow sigh is unmistakable, like a groan from a tiny, cranky old man.

"Tree humor," I explained, just in case Bongo had missed it, although of course she hadn't. Bongo misses nothing. "Because, you know, I'm so tall."

"Really, Red?" Bongo stretched, admiring her lustrous blue-black wings. "That's the best you got for me this morning?"

"Maybe you'd appreciate my joke more if you weren't so sensitive about your stature," I teased.

"Corvids don't give a flying tail feather about height," Bongo said. "Smarts. Wiles. Trickery. Cunning. That's what counts in our neck of the woods."

"Corvids" is a fancy name for birds like crows, ravens, jays, and magpies. Bongo says she's too classy for a label as common as "crow."

A soft wind tickled my branches. Spring, that old rascal, was teasing us with the promise of warmer days.

"The truth is," I said, "it doesn't matter what size you are, Bongo. We grow as we must grow, as our seeds decided long ago."

"Red. Way too early in the morning for the Wise Old Tree routine." Bongo gave me a gentle peck. "Although, you're right. It doesn't matter how tall you are." In a fluttery blur, she sailed to a telephone pole far above my leafy canopy. "Not when you can *fly*, pal."

At almost the same moment, Samar and the boy

who lived in the green house, Stephen, stepped onto their porches. Both had backpacks. Both looked eager to greet the day.

Their eyes met. Stephen nodded—just a flicker—and Samar nodded back. Not a hello, exactly. Just an acknowledgment.

Stephen ran off toward the elementary school down the street, but Samar hesitated. "Hello," she called softly.

Right on cue, Bongo replied "Hello," as she did every morning, sounding just like Samar.

Bongo can also do a passable tuba, an impressive Chihuahua, and a fine police siren.

Samar looked up at Bongo, grinned, and headed toward school.

With that, Bongo let loose a hoarse and gleeful caw, and set off to wait for children to arrive at school. She was a regular there. Everybody knew her. She enjoyed annoying the children, and they enjoyed letting her annoy them.

Bongo especially liked to untie shoelaces. While

the children were busy retying them, she would snatch treats from their lunch bags.

Every now and then, she would even make a polite request. She could say "Chip, please," "No way," and "You rock," when it served her purposes.

Watching Bongo soar, I considered, not for the first time, my rambling roots. What would it be like to fly? To burrow? To swim? To gallop?

Delightful, no doubt. Sheer joy. And yet. I wouldn't trade a single rootlet for any of it.

It is a great gift indeed to love who you are.

12

By this time, the lanky boy had walked past me, swiveled, and returned. Glancing over his shoulder, he stepped onto the brown lawn that blanketed my roots.

The air changed, quivering the way it will when people are near, with chemicals, with pulsing heat, with human-ness.

And then it happened.

He dug into my trunk with the object in his hand. Fast. Deliberate.

Again he checked his surroundings. An elderly woman crossing the street smiled at him and shook her head. She was probably thinking, "How sweet. I'll bet he's carving a heart with initials in it. Oh, to be young and in love!"

People are under the impression that trees don't mind being carved into, especially if hearts are involved.

For the record: We mind.

I'd never seen the boy before. He was big, maybe a high schooler. It's hard to know with people. With a tree, I can sense to the month, sometimes to the day, its age.

I couldn't tell what he was carving, of course. But I could tell from the determined way he moved that it was meant to hurt.

Not me. Somehow I sensed it wasn't meant to hurt *me*. I was just his canvas.

That said, it's not exactly a picnic, getting hacked

into. Bark is my skin, my protection from the world. Any wound makes it harder to fight off disease and insects.

I wanted to yell "Stop!" To say something. Anything. But of course I didn't. It's not our way.

Trees are meant to listen, to observe, to endure.

He was done quickly. He stood back, admired his work, gave a little nod, and left. As he walked away, I saw the tool clutched in his fist.

A little screwdriver with a yellow handle.

Thin as a twig, bright as a meadowlark.

13

Bongo was the first to see what had happened to me.

She landed at the base of my trunk, head cocked. Dropping the potato chip in her beak, she cried, "I leave you alone for a few minutes, and look what happens! What on earth?"

"It seems someone mistook me for a pumpkin," I

said. When she didn't smile, I added, "Because, you know, I was carved."

"For the millionth time, Red, explaining doesn't make things any funnier."

Bongo flew to my lowest scaffold branch—one of my big, primary limbs. She examined my injury. "Does it hurt?"

"Not the way an injury might hurt you. Trees are different that way."

"I gotta do something," Bongo said.

"There's nothing to be done."

"You've got a major boo-boo. I want to help. You're the Wise Old Tree. Tell me what to do."

"Really, Bongo. Time heals all wounds."

Bongo hates it when I philosophize. She rolled her eyes. (At least I think she did. It's hard to tell with crows. Their eyes are like morning blackberries, dark and dewy.)

"I just hope my bark isn't ruined," I said. "That's my favorite side."

"It's not ruined. Just decorated. Like those tattoos people get." Bongo nudged me with her beak. "Show me who did this. I'll get him. I'll squawk at his window in the middle of the night. I'll dive-bomb him and yank out some hair." She flapped her wings. "No! Better yet! I'll make a deposit on his head. I'll make a deposit on his head every day for a year!"

I didn't ask what kind of deposit. I was quite sure I knew.

"Bongo, dear," I said, "that won't be necessary."

Bongo shifted from foot to foot, something she did when she was working out a problem. "You know," she said, "it's almost time for Wishing Day. Maybe this is some kind of wish. Just a poorly delivered one."

"Another Wishing Day," I repeated. It seemed like we'd just had one. Had a whole year already come and gone? Days have a way of slipping past like raindrops in a river.

"One more round," Bongo said, "of greedy people bugging you with their needs."

"One more round of hopeful people wishing for better things," I corrected.

Wishing Day was always a bit hard on me, and on my residents. Usually the animals and birds stayed away that day to avoid curious hands and endless photographs.

But it was just one day. I understood its history and my role in it. I knew people were full of longings.

A mother tugging a toddler along the sidewalk froze in place when she saw my trunk.

"Mommy, what does that say?" asked her little girl, who was clutching a stuffed toy dog by its bedraggled tail.

The mother didn't answer.

"Mommy?"

They crossed the lawn. The mother stepped close to me. "It says 'LEAVE,'" she finally said.

"Like trees have leaves?"

Gently, the mother traced my cuts with her index finger. "Maybe," she answered. "Maybe like that."

She looked over at the two houses near me. Shaking her head, she tightened her grip on the little girl's hand. "Let's hope that's all it means."

14

Those houses. My houses.

One painted blue. One painted green.

One with a black door. One with a brown door.

One with a yellow mailbox. One with a red mailbox.

For well over a century, I'd stared at them. Prim and proper. Same small size, same boxy shape, same pitched roofs and squat brick chimneys. Architectural siblings.

Long before they were a glimmer in some builder's eye, I was here, right in the middle of things. If my roots stretched past the property line that separated them, well, that's never been my concern. Roots can be unruly. Mine explored the earth below both houses, pirouetted around their plumbing, anchored their foundations.

I spread my shade fairly. I dropped my leaves evenly. I bombed their roofs with acorns in equal number.

I did not play favorites.

Over the years, many families had called those houses home. Babies and teenagers, grandparents and great-grandparents. They spoke Chinese and Spanish, Yoruba and English and French Creole. They ate tamales and *pani puri*, dim sum and *fufu* and grilled cheese sandwiches.

Different languages, different food, different customs. That's our neighborhood: wild and tangled and colorful. Like the best kind of garden.

A few months ago, a new family, Samar's family,

rented the blue house. They were from a distant country. Their ways were unfamiliar. Their words held new music.

Just another transplant in our messy garden, it seemed.

Except that this time, something changed. The air was uneasy. The parents in the green house refused to welcome the new family. There were polite nods between the adults at first, but then, even those vanished.

Other things happened. Someone threw raw eggs at the blue house. One afternoon, a car passed by, filled with angry men yelling angry things, things like "Muslims, get out!" Sometimes Samar would walk home trailed by children taunting her.

I love people dearly.

And yet.

Two hundred and sixteen rings, and I still haven't figured them out.

Our neighborhood had welcomed many families from faraway. What was different this time? The headscarf Samar's mother wore? Or was it something else?

As all this unfolded, busybody that I am, I kept tabs, eavesdropped, observed. I never interfered, though. Trees are impartial observers. We are the strong and silent type.

Besides, what could I possibly do? I had limbs, but they could merely sway. I had a trunk, but it was rooted to the earth. I had a voice, but it could not be used.

My resources were limited.

So, too, as it turned out, was my patience.

15

When you're the neighborhood wishtree, people talk. It didn't take long for folks to learn about the ugly word carved into my trunk. People stopped to stare. They gathered in little groups. They grimaced and shook their heads and murmured. By lunchtime, the police had arrived.

I am not, as it happens, a stranger to law enforcement. A pair of calico kittens reside across the street.

They love climbing up my trunk to my uppermost branches. Unfortunately, they don't love climbing back down. In the last two months, Lewis and Clark have been rescued twice by the fire department and three times by the police.

Sandy and Max, the same police officers who'd rescued the kittens just last week, climbed out of their patrol car to check me out. They frowned. They searched the lawn for clues. They talked to passersby and took photos.

"Bongo," I whispered, "I'm an official crime scene."

She was not amused.

The owner of the houses—and, therefore, technically, of me—was the one who'd called the police. Francesca, tall and thin, with short, dove-gray hair, lived across the street. The blue and green houses had belonged to her family for generations.

Francesca was also the owner of Lewis and Clark, my intrepid visitors.

With a grim look on her face, Francesca strode

across the street to talk to the police. Lewis and Clark squirmed in her arms.

"That tree," Francesca said to Sandy, who was taking notes on a little pad. "It's been nothing but trouble for as long as I can remember."

Francesca has never been the sentimental sort. She likes cats more than trees.

To each her own. I happen to like trees more than cats.

"Oh, but people love the wishtree," said Sandy. She looked me up and down. "Although I imagine it's a lot of work for you."

"Every year, the day after Wishing Day, I swear I'm going to cut that thing down," Francesca said.

It was true. But I knew Francesca didn't mean it. She and I went way back.

"The cleanup isn't the worst of it," Francesca continued. "The things people wish for! The craziness! Last year someone wrote *I wish for chocolate spaghetti.* In permanent marker. On a pair of underwear. Tossed it way up high."

"Chocolate spaghetti," Sandy said. "I could get behind that."

"Craziness, I tell you." Francesca stared at me. "It's just a tree, after all. Just a tree."

"Just a tree" seemed a tad unfair. But Francesca looked tired and angry, so I tried not to take it personally.

Sandy closed her notebook. "People believe what they wanna believe. About trees." She stared at the newly carved word. "About people, too."

"What now?" Francesca asked.

"Dunno," Sandy said. "The tree belongs to you, not the new family, and you've been here forever."

Francesca smiled sadly. "S'pose it could be me they're hoping will leave."

They watched Max place a circle of yellow crime scene tape near my trunk, using metal stakes. "Don't think so, Francesca," Sandy said.

Max joined them. He stroked the kittens, who purred loudly. "One problem, in terms of prosecuting anyone," he said, "is the history of this tree. It's almost

May, when people leave their . . . wishes or whatever. Hard to say for sure this isn't part of the whole, you know, tradition thing." He shrugged. "That's assuming we figure out who did this, mind you."

"People are supposed to make their wishes on a rag or piece of paper, not carve it into the trunk," Francesca said. "That's why, back in Ireland, they called these 'raggy trees.' Nowadays, a lot of people just tie a tag around a branch and write their nutty wishes." She shrugged. "In any case, 'LEAVE' is not a wish. It's a threat."

"It certainly is," Max agreed.

Francesca nodded at the cracked and buckled walkways leading to both houses. "Tell you one thing. Wishtree or not, this oak is destroying the walkways. Messing with the plumbing, too. Roots go on forever." She shook her head. "Maybe it really is time to cut it down. No more leaves to rake. No more Wishing Day mess. No more of this . . . unkindness."

Lewis leapt from Francesca's grasp and dashed for my trunk. Sandy tackled him just in time.

"We'll finish up our investigation in a day or two, be out of your hair," Max said. "Then you'll be free to do whatever you want with the tree."

"You know," Francesca said, taking Lewis from Sandy, "my father almost cut this tree down years ago. My mother wasn't having it. Family lore or some such thing. Soft-hearted nonsense." She sighed. "Guess it's up to me."

"Meantime, you keep us posted if anything else happens," Sandy advised.

Francesca headed across the lawn, holding the kittens close. "'LEAVE,'" she murmured. "What a world. What a world we live in."

16

When you're a tree, a phrase like "cut it down" is bound to get your attention.

Francesca had hinted at such things before, but always in jest, after a long October afternoon raking my newly shed leaves into crisp hills. Or after a particularly messy Wishing Day. Or after stepping on my acorns in bare feet.

I felt bad about the walkways. It's an occupational

hazard. To stay alive, I need a vast network of roots. And roots can be surprisingly strong.

"Did you hear that?" Bongo asked, watching Francesca enter her house. "She sounded serious this time."

"I've heard it all before," I said.

"Unfortunately, the newbies heard her, too," Bongo said.

Bongo calls every fresh crop of babies "newbies." She pretends to be annoyed by their antics, but I know better.

"Listen," Bongo urged.

Sure enough, I could hear the baby skunks wailing from their hidden nest under the porch. "But we love Red, Mama!" one of them cried.

"Hush," their mother, FreshBakedBread, scolded. "It's the middle of the day. You're supposed to be asleep. You're crepuscular."

Crepuscular creatures, like fireflies, bats, and deer, are especially active at dusk and dawn.

"Will Red be all right, Mama?" another baby, whose voice I recognized as RosePetal, asked.

All skunks name themselves after pleasant scents. I am not sure if this is because they're a bit defensive about their reputation, or if they just have a sly sense of humor.

"Of course," said her mother. "Red is indestructible."

Bongo looked at me. "See what I mean?"

"Oh, dear," I said. "By tonight they'll all have heard. The opossums, the raccoons, the owls . . . Little Harold will be beside himself."

Harold was the smallest barn owl nestling, and a great worrier.

Barn owls give themselves sensible, no-fuss names.

"I'll talk to everyone," Bongo said. "Calm them down. Tell them not to worry."

"I'm sure things will be fine," I said. "I've seen a lot in my years. The things I've fretted about that have never come to pass! I could write a book." I paused. "In fact, I could be a book." I paused again. "Because, you know . . . paper is made of trees."

Bongo gave a screechy crow-laugh. She didn't even scold me for my lame joke.

That's when I started to worry.

17

As much as I was concerned about the babies' reaction to Francesca's words, I was more worried about Samar. What would happen when she returned from school and saw the word carved into me? Would she think it was meant for her, and for her family, as Francesca and the police seemed to assume?

She came home alone. Ahead of her by a few yards was Stephen.

A reporter from the neighborhood newspaper was waiting on the sidewalk, interviewing people as they walked by. Word travels fast in our parts. Especially when there's yellow police tape involved.

Had they seen what had happened? the reporter kept asking. Had they ever made wishes on Wishing Day? What did they think the word "LEAVE" meant?

The reporter approached Stephen. Did he know why someone would carve "LEAVE" into the beloved local wishtree?

Stephen stared at the reporter. Then he glanced behind at Samar, sending her the shadow of a sad smile. Without answering the reporter, he headed toward his house.

Samar's eyes darted from Stephen to the reporter to me. She ran closer, saw the word, and gasped. She reached a hand toward me, but the police tape put me out of reach.

"Are you a resident?" the reporter asked. "Would you like to comment on the incident?"

Samar didn't say a word. She turned and walked up the sagging steps to the little blue house, her head held high. Standing tall, reaching deep.

18

Around six that evening, Sandy and Max returned. When the police knocked on the door of the green house, Stephen's parents opened it and answered questions. They shook their heads. They shrugged. Then they shut their door and closed the curtains.

When the police knocked on the door of the blue house, Samar's parents opened it and answered questions. They rubbed their eyes. They sighed. Then they, too, shut their door and closed the curtains.

As Sandy and Max headed back to their cruiser, Sandy paused beneath me. "I wonder if we should make a wish," she said. "Might be our last chance."

"I'll tell you what I wish for," Max said. "I wish I didn't have to investigate things like this."

Sandy patted his shoulder. "I wouldn't hold my breath on that one."

As for me, I spent the evening hours reassuring the parents and offspring who called me their home. They weren't just worried about where they would have to move, of course. They were worried about me.

I was worried about me, too. I didn't want to leave the world I loved so much. I wanted to meet next spring's owl nestlings. I wanted to praise the new maple sapling across the street when it blushed red as sunset. I wanted my roots to journey farther, my branches to reach higher.

But that is how it is when you love life. And I could

accept that if my time had come, it had come. After a life as fine as mine, who was I to complain?

I was worried about the babies, though, about their parents scrambling to find new, safe places to line their nests, dig their burrows, hide their winter stashes of acorns.

Most of all, I was worried about Samar.

I don't know why. Perhaps it was because she reminded me so much of another little girl from another time long ago. A little girl I'd managed to shelter successfully.

Francesca's great-grandmother.

Like I said. We go way back.

19

Long after midnight, Samar came to visit me. She wore a blue robe. Her dark curly hair was pulled back in a loose ponytail. Her eyes held moonlight in them.

She sat at the base of my trunk on her blanket. She didn't look at the carved word, or the splinter of moon, or the blue and green houses. She just sat quietly and waited.

It always took a while. But it always happened.

One by one, the babies ventured out to see her.

Harold was first, flapping awkwardly down to the ground. The raccoon babies, You, You, and You, were next. (Raccoon mothers are notoriously forgetful, so they don't bother with traditional names.) The opossums. The skunks. They all came.

Samar sat perfectly still. The babies circled her.

Together they sat in the shimmer of moonlight and listened to my leaves rustle.

Bongo settled on Samar's shoulder. "Hello," she said, in her crow version of Samar's voice.

"Hello," Samar said, echoing the echo.

Bongo squawked and Samar jumped a bit. Even Bongo's quietest caw is a bit on the harsh side. Bongo flew up to my smallest hollow and poked her head inside, her tail feathers still visible. With something shiny in her beak, she returned to the ground in front of Samar. Gently she placed a tiny silver key attached to a long, faded red ribbon in Samar's open hand.

"It's beautiful," Samar whispered. "Thank you."

Bongo bent forward, wings spread, in a sort of bow. It was, in crow circles, a sign of great affection.

I'd seen that key before. Bongo had "inherited" it from her mother. Crows live in extended families, and they pass information across generations. It didn't surprise me that Bongo still had the key, or that she'd decided to give it to Samar.

In the sweet calm, surrounded by everything I loved—moonlight, air, grass, animals, earth, people—I wondered, with a pang, how much longer I would be able to savor such moments.

I wondered, too, if I'd done enough for the world

I loved. It was something I'd asked myself before. But impending death has a way of focusing your attention.

Sure, I'd provided plenty of shade. Made oceans of oxygen for people to breathe. Been a home to an endless parade of animals and insects.

I'd done my job. A tree is, after all, just a tree. Like I'd told Bongo: "We grow as we must grow, as our seeds decided long ago."

And yet.

Two hundred and sixteen rings. Eight hundred and sixty-four seasons. And still something was missing.

My life had been so . . . safe.

Upstairs, a curtain in the green house moved. Behind it, Stephen was just visible, watching us.

I knew what he was thinking. One of the advantages of being a good listener is that you learn a great deal about how the world works.

In Stephen's eyes, in the way he'd looked at Samar that afternoon, I saw something I'd seen many times before.

A wish.

20

After Samar left, I felt restless.

Restlessness is not a useful quality in a tree.

We move in tiny bits, cell by cell, roots inching farther, buds nudged into the sunlight. Or we move because someone transplants us to a new location.

When you're a red oak, there's no point in feeling fidgety.

Trees, as I said, are meant to listen, to observe, to endure. And yet, just once, before I said good-bye to the world, what would it be like to be something other than passive? To be an actor in the stories unfolding around me? Maybe even to make things a little bit better?

"Bongo," I said softly. "Are you awake?"

"I am now," she grumbled.

"I have a question."

"I'll get back to you first thing in the morning."

"How does friendship happen?"

Bongo responded by snoring.

I could tell it was a fake snore. Her real snores are so loud they scare the baby opossums.

"I'm serious," I said.

Bongo groaned. "I dunno. It just happens."

"But *how* does it happen?"

"Friends have things in common," Bongo said. "And there you go. Your answer in five words. See you in the a.m., pal."

I thought about her reply. "But what do you and I

really have in common, when you get right down to it?"

With a loud exhale, Bongo flew to the ground. "Okay. I'm thoroughly awake now, thank you very much. What's this all about?"

"Just an idea."

"Here's an idea for you: Ideas are a bad idea," said Bongo. "Especially if someone is in busybody mode. I'm lookin' at you, Red."

"Back to my question. Why are we friends?"

"Okay, fine. Let me think on it for a minute."

Bongo walked in a slow circle around my trunk, considering.

I love the way birds move, so unlike trees. We bend with the wind. We're graceful and unhurried. Birds, on the other hand, move in flits and twitches. Their heads whip from side to side, as if they've just heard astonishing news.

Bongo paused. "Well, to begin with, you're my home. And I'm your tenant."

"But that's not really a reason for us to be friends. I've had residents I wasn't particularly fond of."

"That squirrel? What was his name? Squinch? The one with bad breath?"

"It's not important."

"Knew it was Squinch."

"Bongo," I said. "Please focus."

Bongo gazed up at me. "We're friends because we're friends, Red. Isn't that enough?" Her voice was small and sweet—not her usual get-to-the-point crow tone.

"You're right," I said. "But suppose two people needed to be friends. How would you make that happen?"

"Maybe . . . get them together, doing something. They yak, share a laugh. Voilà. Friendship. Am I right?"

"Hmm."

"I don't like it when you hmm. Hmm-ing leads to ideas."

"You can go back to sleep, Bongo. Thanks for talking. You're a good friend."

"Likewise." Bongo flew back up to her nest. "Hey, be sure to let me sleep in."

"Bongo?"

"*Now* what?"

"One more thing. Why do you think people can be so cruel to each other?"

"It's not like the rest of us are exactly angels. Last night I saw Agnes eat a whole lizard in one bite."

Agnes, the barn owl who lived with her nestlings in my highest hollow, flapped her wings in annoyance. "Hey, a girl's gotta eat. And you're a fine one to talk, Bongo," she said. "Is there anything crows *won't* eat?"

"My point," Bongo continued, "is that the world's a tough place. Doesn't matter if you're a bunny or a lizard or a kid."

With that, Bongo started snoring—for real this time—but I was still wide awake.

"Ma, what's the horrible noise?" came the startled voice of a baby opossum.

"That's just Bongo sleeping," her mother replied.

Bongo had been right. I was hatching an idea.

She'd always said I was a busybody, not to mention an optimist.

An optimistic buttinsky.

Well, there were worse things.

Trees are the strong, silent type.

Unless we're not.

21

"Bongo," I said early that morning as the last stars faded like weary fireflies, "there's something I need you to do."

"Does it involve potato chips?" Bongo mumbled.

"No."

"Then I'd rather sleep."

"It's about Samar."

"You promised you'd let me sleep in."

"I didn't promise."

"You implied."

"I want to grant Samar's wish."

This roused Bongo. She fluttered down to her favorite branch, the one she'd nicknamed Home Plate. (Bongo likes to watch the kids play softball at the elementary school.)

"Uh, Red, you don't make wishes happen. You're the place where wishes go. You're like a . . . like a leafy garbage can. In a good way."

"For two hundred and sixteen rings, I've sat on my roots and listened to people hope for things. And a lot of times, those wishes never happened, I'm guessing."

Bongo tucked a feather into place. "Sometimes that's for the best. Remember that kindergartner who wanted a bulldozer?"

"I'm passive. I just sit here watching the world."

"You're a tree, Red. That's kind of the job description."

"This is a good wish. And it's a wish I can make happen." I paused. "Well, we can make happen."

"Yeah, I had a feeling that's where this was going." Bongo glided to the ground. "Look, I heard Samar's wish. How exactly are you going to find her a friend?"

"You'll see," I said, hoping I sounded more confident than I felt.

"Red." Bongo paced back and forth. With each step, her head bobbed forward. "We've got more serious issues, pal. Francesca's talking about turning you into toothpicks. And your residents are frantic about where they're going to move if that happens." She came close and nudged me fondly. "Of course, they're worried about you, too."

"I know that."

FreshBakedBread poked her head out from under the porch. It was barely dawn, and only the white stripe running the length of her face was clearly visible.

"I've offered to take in one of the tree families temporarily," she announced. "Preferably the opossums. They're better behaved than the Yous."

"That's very generous of you, Fresh," I said, but I

was interrupted by BigYou, the mother of the three raccoon babies. She was in my large hollow, grumbling under her breath.

"I beg your pardon," she exclaimed. "You, You, and You have excellent manners!"

"They're too . . . inquisitive," said FreshBakedBread. "Always poking their noses where they shouldn't be. Grabbing things with those little paws of theirs."

"Well, at least they don't stink!" BigYou cried. "And your children have paws, last time I checked."

HairySpiders, the mother opossum, peeked out cautiously from her own hollow.

Opossums name themselves after things they fear.

"Stink is in the nose of the beholder," said HairySpiders. "And while I personally think your children have a delightful odor, Fresh, I've already got dibs on the woodpile two doors down. Should anything happen to dear Red." She patted me. "No offense, love. Just thinking ahead, you know."

"No offense taken," I assured her.

"I saw that pile first!" BigYou cried.

"Share the skunk den," HairySpiders said.

"I wouldn't be caught dead in that place!" BigYou exclaimed. "Not now. Now that I know my 'inquisitive' children aren't wanted."

"Well, they are a bit boisterous," said HairySpiders.

"At least my children have spunk," said BigYou. "Your kids faint when they see their own shadows."

"Playing possum is a useful adaptation," said HairySpiders, her pink nose twitching. "The world is a dangerous place. And in any case, we can't control it. It just happens."

"If I may interrupt," came a cool voice from my highest branches. It was Agnes. "There's a nice-looking linden tree two blocks away, just vacated by a gray squirrel family. We're looking at it as a possibility. But there's a tomcat that runs loose there. Collar, no bell, so that's an issue. Also a big, slobbery dog."

"In fairness, all dogs are slobbery," Bongo observed.

"I really think you should all calm down," I interrupted. "Let's not buy trouble. One day at a time, my friends. Who knows what tomorrow may bring?"

The mothers glared at me. I heard a great deal of sighing.

"Too much Wise Old Tree?" I asked.

"Too much Wise Old Tree," Bongo confirmed, as

everyone retreated into their homes in a huff.

"They're all a bit tense," Bongo said. "Worried about your . . . your situation."

"I can see that."

"I'm worried, too," Bongo said in an almost-whisper.

"I know," I said gently. "But every cloud has a silver—"

"Red," Bongo interrupted.

"Sorry."

"There must be something I can do," Bongo said.

"You're a good friend, Bongo. But sometimes all you can do is stand tall and reach deep."

"Red!"

"Sorry," I said again.

"What will I do without you, Red?" Bongo said softly.

"You'll be fine, my friend. I promise."

We both fell quiet.

At last Bongo shook herself, feathers fluffing. "In any case. Maybe not the best time to be granting wishes, is my point."

"Seems to me this is exactly the right time," I replied.

Bongo groaned her little-old-man groan.

She knew I wasn't backing down.

And with that, we began to plan.

22

We executed Plan Number One an hour and a half later, when Stephen headed off to school.

He'd gotten only as far as the sidewalk when Bongo dove straight toward his backpack. Poking at the zipper with her beak, she cawed frantically.

When crows want to be loud, they can be extremely loud.

"What?" Stephen cried. "What is *wrong* with you,

bird?" He dropped his backpack to the ground.

Bongo landed on the backpack, looking up at him hopefully. "Chip, please," she said.

Stephen rolled his eyes. "Seriously?"

"Hello," Bongo said. "Chip, please."

Stephen put his hands on his hips. "Okay. Fine. I've seen you in action, working the bus line."

Bongo hopped to the ground as Stephen unzipped his backpack. "You rock," she said politely.

Stephen pulled out his lunch bag and opened it. "Let's see. I've got a tuna fish sandwich. Carrot sticks—"

But before he could say anything more, Bongo plunged into the backpack, grabbed a sheet of paper, and flew skyward.

"Hey! That's my English homework!" Stephen cried. "Come back here, you thief!"

Bongo flew high into my branches and landed with a victorious caw.

Stephen stalked around the bottom of my trunk, where the yellow police tape encircled me.

"Please, crow," he pleaded. "I'll give you my whole sandwich. Please?"

Bongo perched on the paper, freeing her beak. "No way," she replied.

A few more minutes of grumbling, and Stephen gave up. "Great," he muttered as he grabbed his backpack. "Ms. Kellerman is never going to believe me when I tell her a crow ate my homework."

23

When Samar exited her house, it was time for the rest of our plan.

She paused, as she always did, to say hello, and Bongo, as she always did, said hello back. But this time Bongo surprised Samar by landing on her shoulder and presenting her with a mangled piece of paper.

Samar took it from Bongo. "This has Stephen's name on it. Why on earth do you have it?"

"No way," Bongo said, by way of an answer.

"Well, I'll be sure he gets this," Samar said.

Bongo gave a little caw and headed back to me.

Perfect. A simple plan, beautifully executed.

Samar would give the homework to Stephen. They'd strike up a conversation about the crazy crow in the big oak tree. They'd laugh. They'd share. They'd realize they have a lot in common.

Voilà. Friendship.

It was a great plan.

Except for the part that came just seconds later. The part where Samar noticed a friend of Stephen's walking by. She dashed over and asked him to give Stephen the piece of paper.

And that was that.

"Meddling isn't as easy as I thought it would be," I confessed to Bongo.

"Hey, I did my part."

"You were wonderful," I said. "Well, we'll just have to try again. We don't have a lot of time."

"Red," Bongo said with a sigh, "please don't remind me."

24

That afternoon, we tried Plan Number Two.

"This isn't going to work, Red," Bongo said, strutting back and forth on the lawn.

"Pessimist," I said.

"Optimist," she replied.

Secretly, I had my doubts, though. Our second plan required help from one of the babies.

There'd been much bickering over which baby

would get to assist us—but then, there'd been plenty of bickering ever since Francesca's threat to cut me down. It frustrated me to see my residents, the ones who'd miraculously been getting along so well, turn on one another when faced with a problem.

Granted, it was a big problem. But if I could handle it, it seemed like the least they could do was behave during our last days together.

Bongo flipped a penny she kept in her collection of treasures, and we arrived at our helper: the smallest baby opossum, Flashlight.

"Let me get this straight," said Bongo. "You're afraid of flash—?"

"Shh," HairySpiders hissed. "We try not to say that word around him."

"So what do you actually call him?" Agnes asked.

"He answers to 'Flash,'" HairySpiders explained.

"Well, Flash," said Bongo, "you understand the drill, right? You pretend to be dead. You guys are good at that, right?"

Flash nodded excitedly. "Opossums are the best dead pretenders in the world."

"So you play dead, Samar and Stephen see you as they're coming home from school—"

"We're hoping they come home at about the same time today," I interrupted.

"—and they freak out," Bongo continued, "see the cute little maybe-dead baby, talk about what to do—"

"Are you certain this is safe?" asked HairySpiders. "I'm feeling a little faint just thinking about it."

"We'll all be watching. And Stephen and Samar are smart kids," I reassured her. "They'll know not to touch a sick animal."

"So they go get their parents, call a wildlife rescue place or maybe a vet, and while they're busy," Bongo continued, "little Flashli—er, Flash—runs back to his den. Samar and Stephen come back out, have a good laugh about the vanishing opossum, maybe the parents even get to talking—"

"I really think You would do a better job," BigYou complained. "She's a born actor. Or You or You."

"This has been officially decided," Bongo said firmly. "We flipped the penny, remember?"

"Just saying," BigYou muttered.

Down the street, the school dismissal bell rang. "Places, everyone!" Bongo urged.

"This is totally going to work," I said.

"This is totally going to fail," Bongo said at the very same instant.

25

"And action!" Bongo whispered.

Little Flash waddled out to the middle of the lawn.

He lay down on his side and curled up. He closed his eyes. He drew back his lips, revealing tiny, needle-sharp teeth.

"Perfect," Bongo said.

"Try foaming at the mouth, dear," HairySpiders called.

Down the street, we could see Stephen approaching. Luckily, Samar was just a few yards behind him.

Flash leapt up. "How am I doing, Ma?"

"Wonderfully, my baby," said HairySpiders. "Mommy's so proud of her little bitty opossum!"

"BE DEAD!" Bongo cried.

"Oh, yeah." Flash shrugged. "I kinda forgot, Aunt Bongo."

"I'm not your aunt," Bongo said. "I'm not even a member of your species."

"Well, that doesn't really matter," I chided.

"BE DEAD!" Bongo cried again.

Flash hiccuped.

"Oh, my," said HairySpiders. "He does that when he's nervous."

"How come I can't be dead, Mom?" asked RosePetal.

"NEWBIES, QUIET!" Bongo commanded. "FLASH, STOP HICCUPING, DUDE!"

"Here they come!" I whispered. "Stephen and Samar!"

The hiccups got louder.

"FLASHLIGHT!" Bongo said. "NOW!"

"Don't call him that!" his mother cried.

Flashlight froze. He stopped hiccuping. Foam dripped from his mouth. His half-open eyes were glazed and unseeing.

"The works!" Bongo whispered. "Brilliant!"

Stephen found Flash first. Samar was close behind.

"What should we do?" Stephen asked.

Success, I thought. They were actually talking to each other.

"Don't touch it," said Samar. "It might be rabid. Or it could just be playing dead. I read that opossums will do that."

"I'll go get my mom. Maybe she can call someone."

"Sounds good," said Samar.

To my disappointment, Stephen and Samar nodded at each other and promptly went into their separate houses.

And once again, that was that.

All that work, for just a few moments of conversation?

How, exactly, *did* people make friends? How hard could it be?

Still, I reminded myself, Stephen and Samar had spoken to each other. And that was a good first step, wasn't it?

"Flash?" Bongo called. "Time to go back to your den, buddy. Before they come back."

Flash remained frozen in a little opossum ball.

"Flash?" I called.

"Flash? Baby?" HairySpiders yelled.

"Oh, my," said BigYou. "I don't think your baby's acting."

"My baby! My precious Flash!" cried HairySpiders, and Flash's brothers and sisters began to wail.

"You really should have used one of my Yous," BigYou said.

"FLASH! STOP BEING DEAD!" Bongo yelled. She hopped over to Flash and gently poked him with her beak.

"How dare you peck my son!" HairySpiders yelled. "Flash! I'll save you, baby!"

HairySpiders dashed out of her hollow, scrambled down my trunk, and promptly fainted.

"Oh, great," said Bongo. "Just fantastic. Like mother, like son. What now, Wise Old Tree?"

"You grab Flash," I instructed. "FreshBakedBread and BigYou, can you rescue HairySpiders? Pull her over to Fresh's den, under the porch."

"HairySpiders called my children 'boisterous,'" BigYou said.

"BigYou said my children stink," FreshBakedBread said.

Over two centuries of life, and I'd hardly ever raised my voice.

This was one of those times.

"NOW!" I commanded, just as the door to Stephen's house opened.

You'd be surprised how fast raccoons and skunks can be when they're motivated.

26

Stephen and his mother eventually gave up trying to find the mysterious baby opossum. Samar watched them from her living room window, but she didn't venture out.

After about an hour, HairySpiders and Flashlight woke up and returned, on wobbly legs, to their den.

And that was that. Again.

"Don't worry," I told Bongo. "Third time's a charm."

"What's that supposed to mean?"

"It's just something people say."

"*Charm*," Bongo sneered. "Did you know that's what people call a bunch of hummingbirds?"

"No, actually."

"Hummingbirds! Which, let's face it, are pretty much just overdressed flies. But a bunch of us crows together, guess what we get to be called?"

"What?"

"A murder! A murder of crows! Can you believe it? A bunch of trees, you're a grove. A bunch of raccoons? A gaze." Bongo flapped her wings. "But crows? We're a *murder*."

"Are you quite finished?" I asked.

"Sorry. I'm worried about you. And I get grumpy when I'm worried." Bongo plucked out a piece of new grass and tossed it aside.

"I have one more plan to get Samar and Stephen talking," I said.

"How about a plan to get you not turned into a picnic table?"

"I can't control everything in life, Bongo," I said gently. "And if I could, what fun would that be? But this little thing. This wish of Samar's. I can make it happen." I hesitated. "At least, I think I can."

"I don't understand why this matters so much to you."

"She reminds me of a little girl I knew a long time ago."

"You're a buttinsky," said Bongo wearily. "But I love you anyway."

She looked at me with something like the crow version of a smile—beak open, head cocked, eyes gleaming. "So what's Plan Number Three?"

27

Once night had fallen, I sent Bongo on her next mission.

"All you have to do is untie Samar's wish," I instructed.

"Oh," she said. "Is *that* all?"

Bongo flew to the low branch where Samar had tied her pink, dotted fabric scrap. She yanked on it with her beak several times. "Easier said than done," she reported.

"You're a crow. Use a tool."

Crows are well-known for making and using tools. They're probably the brainiest birds around.

"Hmm." Bongo poked and considered. "I have a paper clip in my collection. I'll give that a shot."

"It'll never work," Agnes predicted from her nest.

I think owls are secretly a bit jealous of crows.

One by one, heads poked out of my hollows, as well as the skunk den under the porch, to watch Bongo at work.

"What's Bongo doing, Ma?" asked one of the Yous.

"It's called tool use," said BigYou. "No big deal."

"Folks, if you can't say something helpful," I said, "please don't say anything at all."

Bongo returned with a small piece of twisted metal. "Straightened paper clip," she explained. "Found it on the school playground."

With great effort, she managed to slide the straight

end of the paper clip into the knot. But try as she might, she couldn't pull the knot free.

"Almost . . . got . . . it," Bongo muttered between her clenched beak.

"Why is Bongo doing that?" Harold asked Agnes.

"There's no explaining crows," Agnes said.

"Because I asked her to," I said. "Because it's important to me."

With a frustrated groan, Bongo let the paper clip fall to the ground. "It's no use, Red," she said.

"Maybe it's time to give up on this idea," I said with a sigh. "I'm not meant to help. I'm meant to sit here. Just sit."

A gentle wind rippled my leaves. No one spoke.

"Wait just a minute," said BigYou. "Maybe I can lend you a paw."

"You're awfully heavy for that branch," Agnes pointed out.

"Let her try," I said.

Carefully, BigYou inched her way out onto the limb where Samar's wish was tied.

She was indeed heavy, and my branch bowed under her weight, but I held firm. She toyed with the knot, using both front paws. Before long, she'd pulled the strip free.

"Ta-da!" she cried, clutching the fabric in her right paw.

"Well, I did the hard part," Bongo sulked.

"It was a joint effort," I said. "Teamwork. And much appreciated, both of you."

"You have the wish," said Agnes. "Now what, Red?"

"Now we wait until Samar comes to visit," I said. "And then Bongo works her magic."

28

The moon bathed us all in cool blue light as we awaited Samar's nightly visit.

She came out in her robe and slippers. Sitting on her blanket, she waited patiently as the babies scrambled over to see her. Around her neck, she was wearing the beribboned key that Bongo had given her.

"Where's my crow friend?" she whispered, as the

Yous somersaulted in front of her. She looked up into my branches, and I was glad I'd instructed Bongo to hide on Stephen's roof.

Right on schedule, Bongo flew to Stephen's bedroom window. She settled on the sill.

Samar's fabric scrap dangled in her beak.

Carefully, she tapped on Stephen's window.

Nothing happened.

I'd told Bongo to be as quiet as possible. We didn't want Samar to see what we were up to.

Tap, tap, tap. Louder this time.

Still nothing.

Stephen, apparently, was quite a sound sleeper.

Bongo looked at me. Her eyes said "Now what?"

She tried again. *TAP, TAP, TAP.*

Samar started. "What was that?" she asked.

Fortunately, Harold distracted her with an attempt to fly onto her arm. It was more awkward hop than flight, and Samar giggled.

Good going, little Harold, I thought.

Bongo dropped Samar's wish onto the sill. *TAP. TAP. TAP.*

Nothing.

She paced back and forth in front of the window. Then she froze.

Her eyes glinted in the moonlight.

Bongo leaned close to the glass and performed her very best fire engine siren.

By the time Stephen's window flew open, Bongo was already back on the roof, watching her efforts pay off.

Stephen peered out. He rubbed his eyes. He noticed the scrap on his sill. Frowning, he held it up, catching the moonlight in order to read the words written on the fabric.

He looked down at the lawn.

There was Samar, looking up at him, surrounded by an odd collection of baby animals.

"You rock," said Bongo.

29

When Stephen eased out the front door, he was wearing red pajamas and a gray sweatshirt. His light brown hair was mussed, his eyes bleary. The flashlight he was carrying sliced through the darkness.

The babies turned toward him and froze. Their eyes glowed like little moons.

Flash squealed in fear.

Stephen clicked off his light, and Flash seemed

to calm a bit, although he was definitely hiccuping.

"Hey," Stephen whispered.

"Hi," Samar whispered back.

Stephen sat down next to Samar. The babies watched with interest.

"Why do they come to you?" Stephen asked.

"I don't know."

"It's like magic."

"No." Samar shook her head. "I'm just . . . quiet. They like that."

Bongo flew down to Samar's shoulder. "Hello," she said to Stephen, mimicking Samar's voice.

"Wow," he said. "That's amazing."

"Yesterday I heard her imitate a doorbell."

Stephen grinned.

"She gave me this key," Samar said, holding it up. "I don't know what it's for. A diary or a jewelry box, maybe."

"Or the world's smallest door," Stephen joked.

For a while, everyone fell silent. Even the baby raccoons were still.

At last Stephen held out his hand, revealing Samar's wish. "I found this," he said.

Even in the moonlight, Samar's blush was visible. She looked away.

"I'm sorry about that word," Stephen said softly. "The word on the tree. We didn't . . . It wasn't us."

Samar nodded.

"My parents aren't bad people. They're just . . . afraid of things." Stephen shrugged.

"So are mine," said Samar. "I heard my father talking about moving. If we can find a safe place to go." She gave a sad smile. "If there even is such a place."

"I'm sorry," Stephen said again.

The babies, sensing Stephen could be trusted, began to tussle and romp. Harold and the smallest You searched for bugs. RosePetal and her brother, HotButteredPopcorn, played tug-of-war with a long piece of grass.

"I'll miss them," Samar said.

"I hope you don't move," Stephen said.

A light blinked on in Stephen's house. "I should go," he said. "If my parents see me . . . I should go."

"Night," Samar said in a whisper.

Oh, the things I wanted to say to those two! I wanted to tell them that friendship doesn't have to be hard. That sometimes we let the world make it hard.

I wanted to tell them to keep talking.

I wanted to make a difference, just a little difference, before I left this lovely world.

And so I did it.

I broke the rule.

"Stay," I said.

30

The animals gaped at me in astonishment. Even the youngest babies knew about the *Don't Talk to People* rule.

Bongo darted to my top branch. "Red!" she cried in a strangled whisper. "You can't—"

"Oh, but I can," I said. "What have I got to lose?"

"But—"

"As I was saying." I returned my attention to Stephen and Samar.

They were staring at me, jaws dropped, eyes wide, as frozen as Flash had been not long ago.

"We're dreaming," Stephen murmured. "Right?"

"At the same time?" Samar asked. "Is that possible?"

"Pinch me," Stephen said.

Samar complied.

"Definitely felt that," Stephen reported.

"Maybe it was a dream pinch," Samar suggested.

"Excuse me," I interrupted. "I have two hundred sixteen rings' worth of wisdom to convey. And not much time."

Stephen reached for Samar's hand.

"If it's a dream," he said, "at least it's a cool one."

And so I began.

31

I haven't always been a wishtree.

It happened in 1848, long before I was surrounded by concrete and cars, when I was just a few decades old—still a youngster, by red oak standards. No longer a lanky sapling, I was solid and strong, but not anchored to the earth the way I am now.

This was a time, like many other times, when hungry, desperate people sailed on crowded boats to settle here. Many of them ended up, as they always seemed to, in my neighborhood. The blue and green houses were brown then, and filled to overflowing with new arrivals.

Sometimes the newcomers were welcomed. Sometimes they were not. But still they came, hoping and wishing, as people always do.

One of our new residents was a young Irish girl named Maeve. She'd voyaged across the Atlantic with her nineteen-year-old brother, who'd died of dysentery during the trip. Their mother had passed away shortly after Maeve was born; their father, when the children were nine and twelve.

Maeve was solid and plain, but when she smiled, it was like sunshine peeking through clouds. She had a deep laugh, and her hair was as brilliantly red as my finest autumn attire.

Sixteen, alone, and penniless, Maeve shared a tiny room with five other immigrants. She worked night and day, cleaning and cooking and doing whatever she could to stay alive.

Maeve soon discovered she was gifted at caring for the sick. She had no special knowledge. No secret remedies. But she was kind and patient, and she knew how to soothe a fevered brow with a cool cloth as well as anyone. What she didn't know, she was willing to learn.

As time passed, word grew of Maeve's abilities. People brought her their sick piglets and their lame horses, their coughing children and fretful babies. Always she explained that she wasn't sure she could help. But since people in the neighborhood were too poor to go to a doctor, they turned to Maeve.

And since people believed she could help them get better, Maeve tried to live up to their hopes.

When she succeeded, and even when she didn't, patients and their families would leave small tokens for her: a whittled figurine of a bird, a hairpin, half a loaf of bread. Once someone even left a leather-covered journal, with a tiny silver key that opened its lock.

When Maeve was out tending to someone who

was sick, people took to leaving their thank-yous in my lowest hollow. It was still a fresh wound, just a couple of seasons mended. But because it faced the house where Maeve roomed and not the street, it was a safe place to leave a token of gratitude.

That's when I realized that hollows can be a good thing for people, not just birds and animals.

Little did I know just how good.

32

The years passed, and Maeve became as connected to the neighborhood as I was, even as newcomers from other lands added their music and food and language to our little part of the world. No matter where people were from, Maeve cared for them as best she could.

I grew tougher, my older limbs less pliable, my shadow longer. More trees and shrubs joined me, but there was plenty of sun for all of us, and we never wanted for water.

I'd hosted many families by then, mice and chipmunks in particular. My closest confidant was a young gray squirrel named Squibbles. (All squirrel names begin with the letters *S-Q-U*.)

Squibbles was especially fond of Maeve, who often fed the little squirrel table scraps.

Privately, Squibbles and I worried about Maeve. Along the way, Maeve had seen a suitor or two, but nothing much came of those flirtations. She had friends aplenty and work to do from dawn till dusk. Still, she seemed lonely. Sometimes Maeve would sit on the porch steps, watching happy families stroll past, and her eyes would well up with tears. At night, she'd gaze out an open upstairs window, and her sighs would float to us on the breeze, melancholy as the call of a mourning dove.

Often Maeve would sit at the base of my trunk and write in her journal. Now and then she'd read passages aloud. She spoke about the Irish country-side fading into fog. She spoke about her family she'd lost. She spoke about her secret hopes and fears and longings. She had love to give, and no one to give it to.

Maeve adored early mornings, when the world was bathed in mist and the sun was still a promise. She would lean against my trunk and close her eyes and hum a tune from her childhood.

One day, the first day of May, Maeve joined me at dawn. To my surprise, she reached up to my lowest bough and gently tied a scrap of blue-striped fabric in a careful knot.

"I wish," she whispered, "for someone to love with all my heart."

That was my first wish. And the beginning of many more.

33

As the weeks passed, the piece of fabric on my branch drew many comments.

Some of the folks in our neighborhood, the ones from Ireland, would nod knowingly and smile. To them, Maeve would simply say, in her lilting voice, "That's my raggy tree. She's not a hawthorn, but she'll do just fine."

People who'd come here from other lands—and

there were many of them—would frown at the rag, or even reach up to remove it. Maeve would warn, "Don't you be touching my wish, now." Patiently, again and again, she would explain how in her old home, leaving wishes on a raggy tree was a time-honored tradition.

Now and then, people would ask Maeve what she'd wished for. She'd tell them the truth, with a sigh and a wry smile: "Nothing much. Just someone to love with all my heart. Nothing much at all."

Sometimes people would laugh. Sometimes they would roll their eyes. "A wish on a rag won't bring you love, dearie," they would say.

But usually, people gave Maeve a kind smile, a squeeze on the arm, a knowing nod.

And then they, too, would ask if they could add a wish of their own.

34

Another year passed. As May neared, I found myself hosting more scraps of fabric than budding leaves.

Squibbles tried to steal a few fabric strips to line his drey, the nest made of leaves and twigs high in one of my forked branches. I explained he'd have to stick with moss and pine needles until the first of May. Wishes, according to Maeve, could not be touched until after May Day. Then, the ones that weren't carried off in the wind or dragged to the ground by the rain could be removed by people—or by enterprising squirrels.

I suspect she made up that rule for my benefit, so I could grow unfettered, without the weight of wet rags dragging me down.

Just before dawn on the first of May, a young woman approached me. She had dark, wavy hair and wore a tattered gray coat. In her arms was a wrapped bundle.

"Psst," Squibbles whispered to me. "Here comes another wish, Red."

But Squibbles was wrong. There was no wish.

Swiftly, but with great care, the girl placed her bundle in my hollow.

A thank-you for Maeve, I realized. A loaf of bread, perhaps. The girl had probably been one of her patients.

She was gone as quickly as she'd come.

Like a hummingbird, I thought: There, then not there.

Like a gust of wind.

35

Just a few minutes later, Maeve opened the door of the little brown house. She smiled at me, and at the scraps waving in the early-morning breeze.

And then came the cry.

Wail, was more like it.

Coming from . . . me.

Not the meek peep of a wren chick. Not the shy

squeak of a mouse pup. No: This was a cry of righteous indignation.

This was a baby.

36

The baby had a note attached to her blanket. Haltingly, Maeve tried to read it out loud. "Italian," she murmured.

Only later, when she consulted one of her patients, did she understand its meaning:

> *Please give her the care I cannot.*
> *I wish for you both a life of love.*

The baby's hair was black. Maeve's was red.

The baby's eyes were brown. Maeve's were blue.

The baby was Italian. Maeve was Irish.

They were made for each other.

Maeve named the baby Amadora, which meant, in Italian, "the gift of love."

37

Many in the neighborhood didn't approve of an unmarried Irish woman raising an abandoned Italian baby. People talked, as they will, and they tsk-tsked, as they must.

Some people were even angry. They said hurtful things.

They told Maeve that Amadora didn't belong.

They told Maeve she and the baby should leave.

Maeve merely smiled, held Amadora close, and waited and hoped.

On dark nights when hope was scarce, she would sing an old Irish tune, mixed with a newer, Italian song that she had learned from a neighbor. The melody was sweet. The words were silly. The effect was always the same: a smile from little Ama.

Sure enough, the longer Maeve waited, the kinder people grew. And before long, Ama, as she came to be called, was as much a part of our messy garden as all the rest of us.

When Ama was old enough to feed Squibbles and his family, she did. When she was strong enough to climb me, she did. And when she was ready to make wishes of her own, she did.

Ama grew up steady and honest and kind, like her mother, and had babies of her own, and then grand-children and great-grandchildren. Eventually Ama and her husband bought the little brown house, and the one right next to it, and painted them blue and green. Years later, they purchased a house across the street and began to rent the blue and green houses to other families.

The family grew and prospered and argued and failed and loved and laughed.

Always and forever, the laughter kept them going.

And when Ama's grandson had a little girl, he chose a fine Italian name for her, with a fine Irish middle name: Francesca Maeve.

38

As for me, my reputation grew. Hadn't Maeve's wish come true in the heart of a wishtree? Didn't that mean anything was possible?

Of course, as Squibbles often reminded me, I'd had nothing to do with it.

"This isn't a fairy tale, Red," he would say.

But people are full of longings, and decade after decade, the hopes kept coming.

A blessing and a burden it has been, all those wishes, all those years.

But everyone needs to hope.

39

At long last, I stopped talking.

Once the words had spilled out, it was like trying to stop the wind.

In the silence that followed, I felt as if the whole world was holding its breath.

I'd broken the rule.

Stephen and Samar still stared open-mouthed at me. They looked as rooted to the ground as I was.

Neither had uttered a sound while I'd told my story.

The front door to Stephen's house opened. "Stephen?" called his father. "What the heck are you doing, young man?"

Stephen leapt to his feet. "I . . . Here I come, Dad. Um, night, Samar."

"Night, Stephen," she said.

Stephen dashed toward the porch, but stopped halfway. He spun around to look at me.

"Thanks?" he said in a quizzical voice, using the same tone he might have used if Bongo had just made him pancakes.

The door slammed behind him.

Samar stood, holding her blanket to her chest. "I know I must be dreaming," she said.

She headed to her own porch and eased open the door.

"I just wish," she added with a smile, "that I didn't have to wake up."

40

Almost instantly, I regretted what I'd done.

I'd broken the rule. The biggie.

I'd deliberately spoken to people.

And not just a few words. I'd spoken a river of words.

I wasn't like that frog in the mailbox. I hadn't broken the rule accidentally.

I'd broken the rule because I wanted something. I wanted to matter. I wanted to do something meaningful before I died.

I'd done it for myself.

After the shocked babies and their equally shocked parents were safely ensconced in their dens, I admitted my feelings to Bongo.

I waited for her to yell at me.

Bongo is good at yelling.

Extremely good.

You might even say she has a gift.

"Why did I do it, Bongo?" I murmured. "*Why?*"

She flew to Home Plate. She stroked my rough bark with her sleek head.

"You did it, my Wise Old Tree, because you had a story to tell."

"It was foolish," I said. "I'm not supposed to be foolish."

"Not so foolish," Bongo said. "Just hopeful. And everyone needs to hope, Red. Even Wise Old Trees."

41

Morning emerged slowly, heavy with clouds. A light rain had fallen just before dawn, soothing my leaves, if not my mood.

Oddly, the ground felt saturated. Spring was always muddy, of course, but this was unusual. It would make for a messy Wishing Day tomorrow.

An early-rising old gentleman with a bamboo cane approached. He paused to attach a small piece of blue paper to my lowest branch, using a bit of twine. He didn't say his wish aloud, so I couldn't tell what it was. But he had a satisfied smile as he stepped carefully through the soggy grass.

No doubt I'd be seeing more wishes today. Many people came early to grab an easy-to-reach spot.

This would probably be my last Wishing Day. How could it be that my first one, that long-ago day with Maeve, still seemed as fresh in my heart as my conversation with Stephen and Samar from the previous night?

A car slowed to a crawl near the curb. I saw an arm, a blur, and then—*splat*—something hit my trunk.

Splat. Splat. Two more times, and the car roared off with a screech of tires.

Bongo was the first to report on the damage.

"Raw eggs," she said. "I'm assuming that didn't hurt?"

"Didn't feel a thing," I said.

FreshBakedBread, HairySpiders, and BigYou ventured out to inspect the situation.

BigYou slipped under the police tape and licked one of the yolks sliding down my trunk. "Mmm," she murmured. "Raw. Just the way I like 'em."

"Hey, Big, share the wealth," HairySpiders snapped as she and Fresh joined her.

Agnes watched from her perch. "I'd much prefer a squirming mouse pup," she said. "It's all yours, ladies."

"What a nice surprise," BigYou said between slurps.

"This is not nice," Bongo said. "This is people at their worst."

"Still," said HairySpiders, licking her paws, "it'd be a shame to let perfectly good egg goo go to waste. One creature's nastiness is another creature's nibble."

BigYou gave a satisfied burp, and the animals scampered back to their homes.

The door to Stephen's house opened. He walked over to me, saw the eggshells scattered like puzzle pieces, and scowled.

Samar was next, a backpack slung over her shoulder and books clutched to her chest. She leapt over a muddy puddle and joined Stephen.

"Jerks," he muttered, gesturing toward the egg re-
mains. "Sorry, Samar—"

But Samar held up her hand. "Stephen," she said
in a low voice. "Last night."

Stephen nodded ever so slightly, his eyes locked
on me.

"Last night," he repeated, as if they were speaking
in code.

"The tree."

"The tree."

"You heard what I heard?" Samar asked.

"I did."

Samar looked right at Stephen. "You heard . . . the
tree?"

"I heard the tree."

Samar gave a little nod. "So it was, maybe, a trick?
Somebody playing a joke on us?"

"Or maybe we were both sleepwalking at the same
moment," Stephen suggested. He nodded, as if trying
to convince himself. "Yeah. Sleepwalking."

"Have you ever sleepwalked before?"

"No, but there's a first time for everything."

They stood there, looking at me expectantly. Willing me to speak. At least that's how it felt.

I stayed silent. I'd said my piece, and I regretted it.

"Stephen," Samar said softly, "whatever happens, we can't tell a soul about this. Deal?"

"Deal."

"Ever."

"Ever."

Samar sighed. "People would say we were crazy."

"And they'd probably be right," said Stephen.

Samar jutted her chin at me. "Tree? Do you have anything to add?"

I didn't say a word.

Samar and Stephen shared a smile. "Figured it was worth a shot," she said.

They headed off to school together.

Stephen's father came out onto the porch. He was holding a cup of coffee. He caught sight of Stephen and Samar and frowned.

A moment later, Samar's mother stepped out of

the blue house, her keys jangling, a briefcase over her shoulder. She followed her neighbor's gaze.

Both parents watched in silence until Stephen and Samar, walking side by side, disappeared from view.

42

I didn't have much time to mull over my mistake. We had a steady stream of visitors as the hours passed.

Early wishmakers came throughout the day. A little girl who wanted twenty hamsters. The grocer down the street, hoping for a summer of sweet peaches. The usual.

The local reporter returned. She peeked at some

of the new wishes hanging from my boughs and took a photo of the broken eggshells on my trunk.

Sandy and Max came to remove the police tape surrounding me. Francesca joined them. Today she had Lewis and Clark on thin leather leashes. Each cat was wearing an embarrassingly sparkly harness.

Francesca discussed the broken eggs with Sandy and Max, while Lewis and Clark wove around her legs. "I've got a tree cutter coming out later to give me an estimate," Francesca said.

"So you're definitely cutting it down?" Sandy asked, in what I liked to think was a disappointed voice.

"Yep. No question. See that muck? All the water in the yard?" Francesca pointed at the soggy lawn. "Plumber told me this dang tree is plugging up some of the pipes. Least bit of rain and the yard turns into a giant mud puddle."

"Still, people are going to be sorry to see it go," Max said. He reached for Clark's leash and tried to unwrap Francesca.

"I know. It's a good old tree. But sentiment doesn't pay the plumber."

Sandy grabbed Lewis while Francesca attempted to unknot herself from the leashes. "What about the animals and birds that live in the tree?" she asked.

"Ah, that's where I'm using the old noggin," Francesca said. "Every year, the opossums and owls and such vacate the premises on Wishing Day. Strangest thing. It's like they know what's coming." She hopped over the web of leashes. "S'pose they don't like being disturbed. In any case, I'm hoping the cutters will come late tomorrow afternoon. Most of the wishing will be done by then."

"What will you do with all the wishes?" Sandy asked.

"Put 'em in the trash when no one's looking. That's what I do every year. Whole thing's nonsense anyway."

Max and Sandy looked at me sympathetically.

"I know. I know. I don't have a sentimental bone in my body." Francesca paused to address the cats, who were yanking her in opposite directions. "If dogs can do this, why is it such a challenge for you two?"

She turned her attention back to the police. "But it's time. More than time."

"Well, we're going to swing by tomorrow, keep an eye on things. No lead on the person who carved that word. But with the eggs, and people just generally riled, and the cut-down . . ." Sandy shrugged. "Couldn't hurt to have us keep an eye on things."

"Thanks," Francesca said. "Not necessary, but I appreciate it."

Lewis and Clark caught a glimpse of Bongo, and lunged for my trunk. "Whoa, you crazy felines!" Francesca cried, reining them in.

They hissed at Bongo. She spread her wings menacingly and let out her most ferocious caw.

Lewis and Clark retreated for the safety of Francesca's arms. Once again she was a tangled knot of leashes and cats.

Sandy smiled. "Maybe leave the cats home tomorrow, Francesca."

43

That afternoon, I met my executioners.

Not having teeth, I've never really understood the fear people seem to have of dentists. (I've overheard conversations where the words "root canal" and "cavity" were used, but in tree world, those have different meanings.)

After seeing the tree cutters and their equipment, I understood.

When a truck carrying powerful chainsaws, along with something ominously called a stump grinder, shows up, well, you know you're in trouble.

Mind you, an arborist is a great friend to trees. We need our limbs trimmed just the way you need to cut your fingernails and hair, although for us it's only once or twice a year, and it's called pruning.

I always feel especially elegant after a good pruning.

But pruning is usually done with special shears that look like giant scissors or with a small saw on a long pole. Stump grinders are generally not part of the plan.

It didn't help when three men wearing orange hard hats went to Francesca's door and announced they were from Timber Terminators Tree Service.

"I'm going to make a deposit on those silly hats," Bongo muttered.

"No, Bongo," I said, although the idea was tempting. "Let's wait and see what's what. Maybe they're just here for some pruning."

"You really *are* an optimist."

Francesca walked the men over—this time, without Lewis and Clark—and they discussed costs and timing.

That's right. They talked about cutting me down, even as they enjoyed the shade from my lovely limbs.

Talk about insensitive.

One of the men—he introduced himself as Dave—climbed a ladder to inspect my hollows. Agnes, HairySpiders, and BigYou eyed him warily, ready to defend their babies.

"You've got some critters here, ma'am," he reported.

"Yes, yes, I know," Francesca said. "Every year like clockwork."

Bongo flew up to a spot near Agnes. "Just one deposit," she said under her breath. "That's all I'm saying."

"Situation like this, we'd generally advise cutting in late fall. Less likely to disturb any nests."

"I've got that covered." Francesca nodded, hands

on hips. "Animals and birds hightail it outta here every May first. Wishing Day, you know."

Dave scratched his stubbly chin. "Wishing Day?"

"People make wishes, put 'em on the tree. Animals and birds don't like all the noise. If you could do this tomorrow afternoon, the timing would be perfect. You work on Saturdays?"

"Sure do." Dave shook his head. "Wishing Day," he murmured. "Now I've heard everything."

Francesca nodded. She patted my trunk. "Yeah. Craziness. Can't believe I've put up with it as long as I have."

44

Early that evening, Francesca stopped by the blue and green houses.

My houses.

One with a black door. One with a brown door.

One with a yellow mailbox. One with a red mailbox.

She knocked on each door. She explained her plans for me.

Both sets of parents said they understood. They would be sorry to see me go. But it would be a relief to see an end to Wishing Day, wouldn't it? And my absence would mean more sunlight in their living rooms and fewer acorns underfoot.

"Okay. At least let me make a deposit on the parents," Bongo grumbled. "More sunlight! The nerve! How about less oxygen, people? Less beauty?"

"Thank you for defending me, Bongo," I said. "But no depositing."

Samar and Stephen were not so understanding.

They ran after Francesca as she crossed the lawn. Samar pulled on her sweater. "You have to listen to us," Samar said. "You can't cut down the tree."

"I can't?" Francesca inquired. "And why is that, dear?"

"Because," Stephen said, panting, "it's *alive*."

"I'm quite aware of that," Francesca said. "It's a common trait of trees."

She paused, peering down at the ribbon around Samar's neck. "Why, I know that key," she said. "I recognize the ribbon."

"A crow gave it to me."

"No kidding? Smart birds, crows."

Samar slipped the ribbon over her head and handed the key to Francesca.

"Oh, I don't want that old thing," she said, giving it back. "You can keep it. It just made me remember . . . It's not important. It opens a diary. My great-great-grandmother Maeve kept a journal after she moved here."

"So that's what it's for," Samar said.

"Where is it?" Stephen. "The journal?"

"Attic, maybe. Or, no. It's probably in the shed behind Samar's house. Got a lot of old family stuff stashed away in there." She gave a wry smile. "Unless it all floated away. Backyard's pretty wet right now. Which, by the way, is one of the reasons it's time for this tree to say good-bye."

Samar wiped away tears. "You don't understand. This tree . . . It's almost like it's human."

"That's sweet." Francesca patted Samar's head. "But honey, it's just a tree." She squared her shoulders.

"Now, I must go feed Lewis and Clark. I can hear them complaining from all the way over here. And I've got a busy day ahead of me tomorrow."

As she moved to leave, Stephen stepped in front of her. "Before you go," he said, his voice firm, "just listen."

He turned to me. "Say something," he instructed.

"Please, tree," Samar pleaded.

I kept silent.

What more was there to say?

Francesca looked from Stephen to Samar and back again. "Children," she said, "perhaps those video games you like to play have addled your brains."

"Talk, tree," Stephen said.

Silence.

"It *can* talk," Samar told Francesca. "Real words. It told us a story about Maeve."

Francesca, for just a moment, hesitated. She looked at me. "You mean metaphorically, of course. The tree seemed to talk to you. The leaves whispered and so on."

"It told us about the hollow. And the baby."

Francesca blinked. "The baby."

"Yes," Samar said. "The abandoned baby."

Again Francesca paused. "Of course, I've told that family story before. You probably heard it from a neighbor."

Stephen shook his head. "We heard it from the tree."

"Oh, my," said Francesca. She waved a hand in front of her face. "You're wearing me out, you two. I am so very glad my parenting days are behind me. Listen here. You get a good night's sleep. Understand? Or maybe some counseling."

As quickly as she could, Francesca made her way across the lawn, her shoes caked with mud.

"Francesca?" Stephen called.

"It's just a tree, dears. Repeat after me: It's just a tree."

"I was wondering if we could look for that diary."

She glanced over her shoulder. "Maeve's journal? Be my guest. If it's not underwater by now." She held up her palms. "Just . . . no more tree craziness. You hear?"

When Francesca was back in her house, Stephen and Samar looked at me accusingly. "Why didn't you talk?" Samar demanded.

Because it was foolish.

Because I wasn't supposed to.

Because.

Looking defeated, Stephen and Samar trudged away. They hadn't gone far when Samar paused and turned to Stephen.

"Something happened today," she said. "People at school were being . . . weird. Talking about me, whispering. Passing notes, even." She narrowed her eyes. "You didn't tell anyone, did you? About what happened last night?"

"Of course not."

"Then I wonder what was going on."

"You're probably imagining things."

"I don't think so. I mean, I'm used to people talking about me. Being mean. But this was different."

"Things aren't always what they seem." Stephen smiled sympathetically. "Come on. Let's go check out that shed."

I watched the two of them head toward Samar's backyard. They were talking. Laughing. Becoming friends, perhaps.

Maybe I hadn't been so foolish, after all.

45

Trees don't sleep, not like people do, or animals.

But we do rest.

Unfortunately, that night rest eluded me.

I was filled with questions about the coming day, of course.

But most of all, I didn't want to miss a moment of what little life I had left.

I wanted to drink in the stars.

I wanted to feel the fuzzy wings of the owlets.

I wanted to stretch my roots just a tiny bit farther before the night was through.

I wanted to indulge in some quiet contemplation about life and love and what it all meant.

I wanted to philosophize.

"I've been thinking," I said to Bongo. "There's no point in my worrying about tomorrow. It will come soon enough."

"Red," Bongo said.

"Too much Wise Old Tree?"

Bongo paused. She looked at me for a long time.

"Never," she said. "Never, ever too much Wise Old Tree."

Bongo settled onto Home Plate. The world was quiet and calm.

"Want to hear a tree joke?" I asked.

"Is it funny?"

"Probably not," I admitted.

"Then probably no."

"What's a tree's least favorite month?"

"I dunno. What month?"

"Sep-timber." I paused. "Because, you see—"

"Red," Bongo interrupted. "As always, no need to explain."

We didn't speak much after that. Turned out I didn't need to talk about life and love and what it all meant.

It was enough to watch the sky freckled with stars, to smell the sweet wet earth, to listen to the beating hearts of the little ones I could keep safe, at least for one more night.

46

Saturday morning dawned clean and cool. Even before the sun made itself known, the animals and owls departed the safety of my limbs.

Each family had found a new home, all in nearby trees on the same block. The skunks were going to remain under their porch. It made me happy to know that everyone would be staying in the neighborhood.

One by one, they nuzzled me, whispering their good-byes. The babies sniffled, especially Harold and RosePetal and Flashlight. The parents tried to put on brave faces, but their trembling voices gave them away.

It was awful. But I was glad to get it over with.

I've always hated good-byes.

Bongo, for her part, insisted on staying with me to the bitter end.

I knew better than to argue with her.

By six in the morning, Stephen and Samar were sitting together on Samar's porch.

By seven, Sandy and Max had arrived. They parked across the street and sat in their cruiser, sipping coffee and eating doughnuts.

By eight, three local reporters had arrived, armed with microphones and fancy equipment. They took video of the word "LEAVE." They talked about its meaning, about how it had changed the feel of a neighborhood.

They also talked about me, the doomed wishtree.

I didn't like the word "doomed."

But I had to admit it was accurate reporting.

Francesca came at eight thirty, carrying a cup of tea and dragging a small wooden ladder, the one she put out every year for the wishmakers. She went back home and promptly returned with Lewis and Clark on their kitty leashes.

They were not cooperative.

And then the wishes began.

A toddler on her dad's shoulders, reaching high.

An old woman, aided by two young girls.

Neighbor after neighbor, many of whom I'd seen pass by over the years.

Wish after wish after wish.

Some on scraps of colorful fabric.

Many on paper, tied with a ribbon or a string.

A few socks.

Two t-shirts.

And one pair of underwear.

At first, people came in small groups, or one by

one. But then something changed. The trickle of people became a deluge.

Many of them were kids from the elementary school. But there were parents and teachers, too.

A dozen kids. Fifty. A hundred and more.

Every person seemed to be carrying an index card. Each card had a hole punched in it, with a piece of string looped through the hole.

Stephen high-fived many of them. Hugged his principal. Waved to his teacher.

Samar just sat on the steps with her parents, a quizzical expression on her face.

One by one, the children tied their wishes to me. The principal and assistant principal and janitor and teachers all helped.

My boughs had never been more laden.

My heart had never been more hopeful.

Because as each child, as each neighbor, as each stranger, placed a wish upon me, they looked at Samar and her parents and said the same thing:

"STAY."

47

Within an hour, I was covered with the word "STAY."
Extra wishes lay on the ground beneath me, piled like
blossoms. Wishes made their way onto the porches,
the railings, the sidewalk.

After two hundred and sixteen rings, I thought I'd
seen it all.

Turns out, you're never too old to be surprised.

Soon it became clear that the "STAY" wishes had

been Stephen's idea. With the help of his teacher, Stephen's whole class had secretly worked much of the previous school day making the index cards. Word spread quickly about the project. Before long, the whole school had joined in.

"So this was your idea?" Samar asked Stephen.

"I had a lot of help," he said. "It's a miracle we kept it a secret from you."

Samar looked over at her parents. "I don't know if this will change anything," she said.

Stephen looked over at his parents. "Me either."

"Thank you, though," Samar said. "For trying."

Stephen started to reply, but just then, the Timber Terminators truck pulled up.

The end of my story was coming.

Well, it had been a beautiful story. How lucky was I to have seen a day like today?

But Stephen and Samar weren't giving up so easily. They ran straight to Francesca, who was busy untangling the kittens wound around her right leg.

"Please," Samar begged, "you can see how much people love the wishtree. Please don't cut it down."

"Child," Francesca said firmly, "it's time."

Stephen pulled something from his jacket pocket. It was a small leather-bound journal.

"So you found it," said Francesca. "In the shed?"

"Yep," said Stephen, handing the worn diary to her.

"It's a little damp," said Francesca.

Samar pressed the key, its long ribbon dangling, into Francesca's palm. "You should read it."

"Maybe someday."

"How about now?" Stephen urged.

Francesca sighed. "You children need a hobby, you know that?"

She put the key in the silver lock, and the journal clicked open. The pages were yellow, the ink faded. "Let me guess. It's about a tree that can talk."

"Actually, it's about this neighborhood," Stephen said. "It's about us."

"Please?" Samar said.

"Dear, it won't change anything," Francesca said.

"Please," Stephen said.

"Oh, fine." Francesca rolled her eyes. "Gotta wait for the tree guys to finish getting set up. Sure. I'll glance it over. Maybe then you'll leave me in peace."

Dragging Lewis and Clark behind her, Francesca went to Samar's porch, sat on the top step, and began to read.

48

It isn't easy cutting down a big tree.

It takes careful planning and people who know what they're doing.

I'd seen neighboring trees cut down. I knew how things went.

While Sandy and Max moved people to a safe distance, Stephen's parents watched from their porch and Samar's from theirs. Meanwhile, the tree people put ropes around my trunk and consulted with one another.

A man and a woman carried over a huge chain-saw, followed by the stump grinder.

The grinder looked a little like a hungry animal.

Actually, it looked a *lot* like a hungry animal.

"All those critters gone?" Dave called to Francesca.

"Haven't seen any," she answered.

Dave climbed a ladder and peered into my hollows as well as he could. He didn't seem to notice Bongo, who was hiding deep in the owls' former home.

I sat patiently, awaiting my fate, while around me the world buzzed. A huge crowd, filled with old neighbors and new friends, had gathered, it seemed, to see me off.

Near the curb, some kids were making music.

I don't know if it was good music. But it was, most definitely, loud music.

I realized it was the garage band Bongo liked.

The whole thing was almost like a party. A going-away party.

There it was, surrounding me: my wild and tangled and colorful garden.

It wasn't such a bad way to leave the world, I decided.

Not bad at all.

49

Dave had a megaphone, and through it he reminded the crowd to stay behind the barriers that had been erected.

"This is a big tree, folks," he said. "And when it goes, we don't want anyone else going with it."

"Bongo," I said in a voice that only she could hear, "you need to get to a safe place. You heard him: I'm a big tree. You don't want to be in the way when I fall."

"I'm not going anywhere," she replied in a stubborn whisper. "Don't worry about me. I'll be fine. But I'm staying with you, Red. And that's final."

Dave turned to his workers. "Okay. Let's get this show on the road."

"Please, Bongo," I said, softly but urgently.

The saw moved closer.

I waited, expecting to hear the painful roar of the chainsaw engine.

Instead, a small but intense sound filled the air, something like a puppy growl mixed with a kitten hiss.

It was a baby opossum.

Darting through the huge crowd, across the muddy lawn, past Dave and his crew, around the massive saw, beneath the stump grinder, and finally, triumphantly, up my trunk, was none other than Flashlight.

He climbed straight to his former hollow and settled there, his tiny head poking out. He was panting and trembling and hiccuping. But he did not seem to be in any danger whatsoever of fainting.

"I missed you, Red," he said, in a voice so small that only Bongo and I could hear it.

"Hold off on the saw!" Dave yelled. "Some dang animal just ran up the trunk."

Bongo popped out of her hollow. "Flash!" she hissed. "You can't be here! It's dangerous. They're about to . . . you know."

"*You're* here," Flash pointed out.

Across the grass streaked HairySpiders, with her other babies trailing. She went straight to the opossum hollow, where she proceeded to scold Flash as she snuggled him close.

In the sky, little Harold suddenly appeared, frantically flapping his wings like a fuzzy butterfly. Agnes and the rest of her brood followed. They settled into their old home as if they'd never left.

Bongo moved to Home Plate to make room for the owls.

The Yous came next, trotting across the lawn. Last to join the group was the skunk family, who quickly scrambled up my trunk.

Seven opossums, four raccoons, five owls, and six skunks had waddled, scooted, dashed, and fluttered from their various homes, just to see me off.

My residents.

My friends.

The crowd was delighted. People applauded. They cheered. They laughed.

Francesca, straining to get a look, accidentally let go of the kittens' leashes, allowing Lewis and Clark to escape.

They ran straight to me, clambering up my trunk to join the gang.

It wasn't all perfection. The babies and parents were grumbling, but softly enough that none of the humans could hear.

"Ouch!" muttered HotButteredPopcorn.

"Your tail is in my mouth!" cried one of the Yous.

"You smell like skunk!" someone complained.

"I *am* a skunk," came the reply.

"Mom?" asked Harold. "Should I be afraid of a cat?"

"As a rule, yes," said Agnes. "But this is a special circumstance."

It took some effort, but eventually the entire group settled in together above the highest wishes. They gazed down calmly at the fascinated crowd below.

One of the tree cutters took off his helmet and scratched his head. "This just don't happen," he said to Dave. "Those animals oughta be eating each other."

"It's some kinda crazy critter miracle," said another worker. He pulled out his smartphone. "This is going on Facebook."

Lots of other people seemed to have the same idea. Cameras clicked away. Ignoring the barricades, the reporters dashed over, microphones extended, as if they were hoping to interview the animals.

Bongo, always a bit of a ham, was happy to comply. "Chip, please," she said to the microphone waving beneath her.

Dave gestured helplessly at Francesca. "What is up with the menagerie, lady? How are we supposed to cut this tree down?"

Francesca, wiping away tears, stood. She put her arms around Stephen and Samar. Slowly, they made their way across the muddy grass.

When she reached me, she pulled a bookmark from Maeve's journal before handing the book to Stephen. It was a strip of cloth made of blue-striped fabric, frayed and faded.

Maeve's wish.

Carefully, Francesca tied it to my lowest branch, already crowded with wishes. She stared, long and hard, at the animals. Lewis and Clark purred happily.

The crowd quieted. The only sound was the rustling of my leaves.

Finally Francesca spoke. "Look. I don't do speeches. That's not my way." She patted my trunk. "But here's the thing. Until today, I'd almost forgotten how important this old tree is to my family story.

And from the look of it"—she pointed to my residents—"it's important to a few other families as well."

Many people smiled. A few laughed.

"I hate this word," Francesca continued, running
her hand over my carved bark. "Hate it. My great-
great-grandmother Maeve would have hated it just as
much. Here in this neighborhood, we're better than
this." She looked over at Samar's parents. "We don't
threaten people here. We welcome them."

Francesca reached for Samar's hand. "This tree is
staying put. And I hope your family will, too."

50

That night, many hours after the crowd had scattered, Samar slipped out the front door of the little blue house. Stephen, who'd been watching from his bedroom window, joined her moments later. They sat, silent, beneath my wish-laden boughs.

The slightest breath of wind sent the index cards fluttering like huge moths. Moonlight was everywhere, it seemed: on the wishes, on my branches, on the downy-headed owlets, in the upturned gazes of Stephen and Samar. How beautiful we all were, bathed by the soft and silver light.

"Do you think your family will stay here?" Stephen asked. "After everything that's happened?"

"I don't know," said Samar. "I hope so."

The breeze kicked up. Cards chattered. Ribbons danced. A scrap of notebook paper, loosely tied with red yarn to my lowest branch, broke free.

Samar snatched it as it swooped past. She squinted at the scribbled writing. Then she stood, carefully tying the paper back onto my branch.

"What was the wish for?" Stephen asked.

"An invisible robot that does homework."

"Seems unlikely."

"True." Samar leaned against my trunk and smiled. "But then, so does a talking tree."

51

If this were a fairy tale, I'd tell you there was something magical about that Wishing Day. That the world changed and we all lived happily ever after.

But this is real life.

And real life, like a good garden, is messy.

Some things have changed. Some things haven't. Still, optimist that I am, I'm feeling hopeful about the future.

Samar's parents decided not to move, at least not for a while.

Stephen and Samar have become good friends. Sometimes they do their homework at the base of my trunk.

Their parents still don't talk to one another.

I'm not sure they ever will.

The police never found the boy who carved "LEAVE" into my trunk. But a couple of weeks ago, I saw him sauntering by. I pointed him out to Bongo.

Let's just say she made a very large deposit that day.

All my residents are back where they belong, safe in their hollows.

They still argue sometimes. But they haven't yet eaten one another.

Francesca applied to the city to make me a "heritage tree." That means I'm protected forever.

She's also on a first-name basis with a local plumber, who's learning to deal with my pushy roots.

Lewis and Clark still haven't figured out how to walk on leashes.

Bongo's made a new friend. His name is Harley-Davidson. I suspect we may have some crow newbies in our future.

As for me, I promised Bongo I will never be a butt-insky again. I told her that my meddling days are over.

And yet, here we are, you and I.

What can I say? I'm more talkative than most trees.

Still, if you find yourself standing near a particularly friendly-looking tree on a particularly lucky-feeling day, it can't hurt to listen up.

Trees can't tell jokes.

But we can certainly tell stories.

acknowledgments

My eternal gratitude to the remarkable people who helped *wishtree* take root:

- The amazing Jon Yaged, president of Macmillan Children's Book Group, and Jean Feiwel, publisher extraordinaire of Feiwel & Friends, for the welcoming garden

- The brilliant team of Rich Deas, senior creative director, Liz Dresner, senior designer, and Charles Santoso, illustrator par excellence, for bringing Red's world to beautiful life

- Starr Baer, my wonderful production editor, for her TLC, and Gleni Bartels, my wise copy editor, for knowing when to prune

- The fabulous Alison Verost, Caitlin Sweeny, Mary Van Akin, Robert Brown, and Tiara Kittrell, MCPG Marketing and Publicity, for their irrepressible enthusiasm as they help books flourish season after season

- Dr. Lisa Leach, dear and brilliant friend and my go-to expert for all things botanical

- Elena Giovinazzo, my incomparable agent at Pippin Properties, for her unflagging support in all kinds of weather

- Most important, *wishtree* would not have happened without Liz Szabla, greenest of green editorial thumbs, who provided endless nurturing and boundless wisdom in order to make this story blossom. In the wild and tangled and colorful garden that is publishing, you are indeed a treasure.

- Finally, having exhausted my gardening metaphors, all my love and thanks to my wonderful family, especially my children, Jake and Julia, and my husband, Michael.

  You're everything I've ever wished for. And then some.